GW00726952

PRIVATE NOSE

"My...my curtains weren't quite closed," gulped Amelia.
"Suddenly I could see this white shape."

PRIVATE NOSE

Written by
JOHN ROBERT TAYLOR

Illustrated by
EMANUEL SCHONGUT

WALKER BOOKS
LONDON

For Sarah

First published 1989 by
Walker Books Ltd, 87 Vauxhall Walk
London SE11 5HJ

Text © 1989 John Robert Taylor
Illustrations © 1989 Emanuel Schongut

First printed 1989
Printed in Great Britain by
Richard Clay Ltd, Bungay, Suffolk

British Library Cataloguing in Publication Data
Taylor, John Robert
Private nose.
I. Title   II. Schongut, Emanuel
823′.914[J] PZ7

ISBN 0-7445-0819-3
ISBN 0-7445-0833-9 Pbk

CONTENTS

*The lion's huge teeth crunched
through the buffalo bones.*

THE CASE
OF THE
MISSING BEAR

The mighty jaws crashed together. The lion's huge teeth crunched through the buffalo bones as if they were biscuits. The lion swallowed.

"Jack, dear," said Mrs Watson. "Don't eat with your mouth open. I don't want to see your cornflakes. Or hear them."

"Has anyone seen Oxford?" Mr Watson said. He spread some marmalade on his toast. "That cat treats this house like a hotel."

Jack put down his spoon. "She's asleep in the garden. Can I have some toast now?"

His mother nodded. Jack put two pieces on his plate. His father raised his eyebrows.

"I'm not being greedy," Jack said quickly. "The other bit's for LT."

This was an old joke. LT stood for Little Teddy. When Jack was younger, he used to take LT everywhere. According to Jack, LT was always hungry.

"Our new neighbours are moving in to-day," Mrs Watson said. "Mrs Patel told me."

"Have they any children?" Jack asked.

"I think there are two – a girl and a boy. But they may not be the same age as you." She looked across the kitchen table at Mr Watson. "You'll never guess what their surname is. Holmes!"

Mr Watson laughed. "So the Holmeses and the Watsons will be living next door to one another!"

"Why's that funny, Dad?"

"There are some famous stories about a Holmes and a Watson." Jack's father looked at his watch. "I'll have to run or I'll be late for work. I'll put the dustbin in the front garden."

It was Thursday – the dustmen always came on Thursday.

After breakfast Jack went upstairs to his bedroom. It was a little room at the front of the house. LT was sitting on the windowsill. He was wearing a grey woolly hat and a blue jersey.

Jack played with his train, but he kept an eye on the road as well. He wanted to be the first to see the Holmeses.

The house next door had been empty for six weeks. Before that an old couple had lived there. The Holmeses sounded much more interesting.

A red car and a blue and orange removal van drew up outside.

As Jack and LT watched, four people got out of the car. The man had pink and white skin. The woman had dark brown skin. The boy and the girl had light brown skin. The boy was so old that he was nearly grown-up; and the girl looked a bit older than Jack.

Jack enjoyed watching the removal men. They carried beds and sofas and armchairs as if they were as light as feathers. He didn't see much of the new neighbours because they were inside the house. After a while the boy rode off on a bicycle with racing handlebars.

The girl came out into the garden for a few minutes. She looked up at the Watsons' house. Jack ducked back and moved LT from the windowsill. He didn't want the girl to think he was babyish. After all, he didn't really play with LT any more.

The van drove away long before dinnertime. Mrs Watson said she was going to say hello to the Holmeses and see if they needed anything.

Jack went with her. By mistake, he brought LT downstairs as well.

"Are you taking LT?" his mother said in surprise.

Jack felt embarrassed. Of course he wasn't. He left LT in the front porch, on the shelf where the empty milk bottles went.

The Holmeses' house was like the Watsons' but the other way round as if it was in a mirror. Mr Holmes opened the door. Behind him, Mrs Holmes was kneeling on the floor with her head in a packing case. She pulled out her head and smiled at them.

Mrs Watson introduced herself and Jack.

"Holmes and Watson!" Mr Holmes grinned. "I expect the police will want us

Jack left LT in the front porch, on the shelf where the empty milk bottles went.

*Jack knew what to do. He climbed up the
apple tree and on to the top of the wall.*

to help them!"

Everyone laughed. Jack joined in. He wished someone would explain what was so funny about Holmes and Watson.

The Watsons didn't stay long because Mr and Mrs Holmes were very busy unpacking. Mrs Watson invited the whole family to come round for coffee on Saturday morning. Jack felt disappointed because the girl wasn't there.

When they got home, Jack went right to the end of the back garden to play football. He kicked the ball very hard against the wall, and it bounced back at him. It was almost as good as having someone to play with.

He kicked the ball twelve times, and twelve times it came bouncing back. But on the thirteenth kick, his foot slipped. The ball shot up in the air and sailed over the wall into the Holmeses' back garden.

Jack knew what to do. He climbed up the apple tree and on to the top of the wall. It was a short drop down to next-door's compost heap; then there was a shorter drop to the ground. No one could see you from the house.

Just as Jack was about to jump, a voice said, "What do you think you're doing?"

It was the girl. She was standing by the garden shed and she wasn't smiling. In her hand was Jack's ball.

"Hello," Jack said. "Sorry, I kicked my ball over."

"Catch!" She threw it to him. "What's your name?"

"I'm Jack," Jack said. "What's yours?"

"Saturday Holmes."

"Saturday? But that's what comes before Sunday. It's a *day*."

"It can also be a person's name. *Everyone* knows that."

"Oh," Jack thought for a moment. "Do you want to come and play football?"

"No." Saturday sniffed. "I've got something more important to do."

She turned and walked away. Jack climbed down the apple tree.

Oh dear, he thought, I messed that up. She must have thought I was making fun of her name.

He wondered what she had to do that was so important.

Playing football wasn't such good fun as it had been. Jack kicked the ball into the rhubarb and went back to the house. He wished that Saturday had been nicer. He was getting bored with playing by himself. That was the trouble with school holidays.

Jack decided to take LT upstairs. He walked round to the front garden. The dustbin had been emptied, and its lid was lying on the path.

But the bear wasn't on the shelf in the porch.

Jack ran into the house, down the hall and into the kitchen.

"Mum," he said. "Did you take LT upstairs?"

His mother was sitting at the table, putting a new plug on the electric kettle. "Isn't he in the porch?" she said.

"No. I've looked there."

"Well, he can't have gone far." Mrs Watson screwed up the plug. "Perhaps he fell off the shelf. Perhaps you took him down the garden when we got back from next door. Perhaps you – "

"But I *didn't!*" Jack said.

Jack looked in the porch. He looked in the garden. He even looked in the house. But there was no sign of LT.

He went back to the front garden. He couldn't help worrying about LT though of course he was much too old for toys like that. He took out a handkerchief from the pocket of his overalls.

"What's up?" someone said behind him.

Jack looked round, hiding the handkerchief behind his back.

Saturday was leaning on the wooden fence between the front gardens of their houses. The fence was much lower than the brick wall at the back.

"I've lost...something," Jack said. "It doesn't matter."

Saturday looked hard at him. "You sound as if it matters. What is it?"

"It's LT," Jack said before he could stop himself. He was so miserable that he forgot

16

*Saturday was leaning on the wooden fence
between the front gardens of their houses.*

that Saturday might think him babyish. "He's my bear."

"Perhaps I can help," Saturday said. "I'm good at solving mysteries. I've got the Holmes Nose."

Jack stared at Saturday's face. Her nose looked very ordinary to him. It was straight and quite big.

"How can your nose help?" he asked.

"Because it's the Holmes Nose, of course." Saturday climbed over the fence and stood beside him. "Haven't you heard of Sherlock Holmes?"

Jack said that he thought he might have done but he wasn't sure.

"He was the greatest detective who ever lived," Saturday said proudly. "He was the brother of my grandfather's grandfather. I'm a detective too. I decided to start today. That's why I didn't want to play football."

"Oh." Jack felt a little better.

"Now," Saturday said briskly. "You'd better take me to the scene of the crime."

"To the what?" Jack said.

"Where the bearnapping took place."

Saturday tapped her nose. "LT must have been stolen. I can smell it. I need to look for clues."

Jack showed her the porch. Saturday got down on her knees and examined every inch of the tiled floor.

"Look what I've found!" she said. "It was between the doormat and the wall. Does it belong to the missing bear?"

She held up LT's grey woolly hat.

"Yes, it does!" Jack shouted. "That proves he's been stolen!"

"Shh!" Saturday said. "I can't hear myself think."

She looked very closely at both sides of the hat.

"Aha!" she said. "Look at this, Jack. It's an important clue."

A ginger hair glowed against the grey of the hat.

"What does it mean?" Jack said excitedly.

Saturday looked down her nose at him. "It means that whoever took LT almost certainly had ginger hair. Who do you know with ginger hair?"

Jack thought hard. "Miss Lines," he said. "She's my teacher at school. And there's Justin Badweather. He's in the class above me. He's horrible. But he's away at his uncle's. And then there's the policeman who lives down the road – he's got a ginger moustache."

Saturday said, "I can't see why a policeman or a teacher should want to steal LT. It's a pity that Justin isn't here. He sounds a good suspect." She looked down the path towards the gate and rubbed her nose. "But luckily I've got another idea."

"Tell me," Jack demanded.

Saturday shook her head. "Not yet. Not until we know more. We need a witness. Do any of the neighbours look out of the window a lot?"

"Mrs Grump does," Jack said. "She's the lady who lives over the road, next door to the Patels. She's always sewing in her front room. Look, she's there now."

They stared at the house opposite. It was freshly painted and had a very tidy garden. To the right of the door was a big bow window. Mrs Grump was sitting there with a sewing machine on the table beside her.

"Come on," said Saturday. "We'll go and question her."

"But...she might be busy," Jack said.

Mrs Grump didn't like children because they dropped sweet wrappers over the fence into her garden. Sometimes she chased them with her broom.

"Are you scared?" Saturday asked. "You have to be brave to be a detective."

"No..." Jack didn't want to admit that he was scared. He thought of something interesting about Mrs Grump. "She's cruel. Once I saw her throw a stone at Oxford."

"She threw a stone at Oxford?" Saturday said. "Don't be stupid. Oxford's *miles* away."

"Not the town called Oxford," Jack said. He saw a chance to get his own back. "Oxford's the name of our cat. *Everyone* knows that."

"If you ask me," Saturday said, "it's a silly name for a cat. Why's he called Oxford?"

"She's watching us," Jack whispered.
"I know," Saturday said loudly. "I'm *not afraid*."

"She's a she. It's because of Oxford Marmalade."

"I still think it's silly." Saturday started walking down the path. "Come on," she said over her shoulder to Jack. "You're not a cowardy-custard, are you?"

Jack caught her up on the pavement. They crossed the road together and opened Mrs Grump's front gate. It was made of iron and painted shiny black. Mrs Grump's concrete path was so clean it almost sparkled. Even her dustbin looked as if it had a bath every night.

"She's watching us," Jack whispered.

"I know," Saturday said loudly. "*I'm* not afraid."

She marched up the path and pushed the doorbell. It chimed a little tune. She waited for a moment and pushed the bell again.

Suddenly the door opened.

"That's enough of your cheek!" screeched Mrs Grump. She was a big fat woman in a black dress. "You'll wear out my chimes if you ring them more than once. Well! Come on! What is it?"

"I'm Saturday Holmes," Saturday said. "We've just moved in."

"Saturday?" Mrs Grump grunted. "Call that a name?"

"Someone stole Jack's bear this morning," Saturday said. "You know, a teddy bear. He left it in the porch when he came round to our house. Did you see anyone going up their front path?"

"No. No one at all," Mrs Grump snapped. She began to close the door.

Saturday put her foot in front of the door. "You're wrong. At least one person must have gone up there."

"Take your foot away! And don't be cheeky." Mrs Grump swelled like a large black balloon.

"I'm not being cheeky," Saturday said calmly. "When we got here this morning, all the dustbins were full. But when Jack asked me to look at the scene of the...at the porch, I mean, their dustbin was empty. I expect yours is too. So the dustmen must have been."

Jack bit his lip. He had suddenly remembered the dustmen's truck – a panda and a rabbit dangled from a wire across the radiator. Perhaps the dustmen thought LT was part of the Watsons' rubbish. LT might now be hanging there as well.

"Pah!" Mrs Grump said. "Of course the dustmen came. They always do on Thursday. I wasn't counting people like dustmen and milkmen and postmen."

"What colour hair did they have?" Saturday asked.

"What colour hair...?" Mrs Grump swelled a little more. "Pah! I couldn't believe my eyes. The young one had his hair dyed green and blue! The other two have grey hair. At least they're normal."

"Thank you, Mrs Grump," Saturday said. "Goodbye."

She and Jack walked quickly down the path.

"And don't forget to close the gate after you," Mrs Grump called after them. "Carefully – or else you'll chip the paint. Pah! Kids! I ask you!"

"Phew!" Jack said when they were back

in the Watsons' garden. "I'm glad that's over."

"All in a day's work for a detective," Saturday said.

She put her hands in the pockets of her jeans and went to look at LT's hat. They had left it on the shelf in the porch. Jack followed her.

"Trouble is," she said, "we haven't solved the mystery. All we've done is prove that *no one* could have stolen LT. The dustmen had the wrong colour hair. The only other people who've been near the porch are you, me and your mum. Unless your mum's got ginger hair – "

"No, I haven't!"

Mrs Watson had come round the side of the house, walking silently on the grass. Her hair was dark and short.

"You must be Saturday," she said with a smile. "Jack, haven't you found LT yet?"

Jack shook his head. He was beginning to think that LT was lost for ever.

"We'll have a look for him after lunch." His mother ruffled Jack's hair. "Cheer up.

We'll find him. It seems to be the sort of day for disappearances. I haven't seen Oxford since before breakfast."

"Oxford," Saturday said dreamily. "Oxford! Why didn't I think of that before?"

"Are you feeling all right?" Mrs Watson asked.

"Oxford! Oxford Marmalade! What colour is your cat?"

"Well, she's a mixture," Mrs Watson said. "But she's mainly – "

"Ginger!" Jack shouted. "Like marmalade!"

Saturday picked up the grey hat with the ginger hair. She looked at Jack. "Where does Oxford go when she wants to be alone? Anywhere in particular?"

Jack cleared his throat. This was awkward. Oxford had a special place, but it was a secret. She wasn't supposed to go upstairs.

"Actually," he said, "Oxford sometimes hides under my bed. When no one's looking."

Sometimes Oxford slept on top of the

27

bed. There was no need to mention that.

"Come on," said Saturday. "Where's your room?"

They ran upstairs and looked under the bed. Oxford was lying there, washing LT with her tongue. Jack wriggled under the bed and rescued him from between Oxford's paws.

"Is he all right?" Saturday said.

Jack nodded. "Just a bit wet."

That afternoon, Saturday and Jack sat side by side on the wall by the apple tree. LT was drying out between them.

Jack's mother had explained that Oxford thought LT was her kitten, and so she was washing him. Mrs Watson had given Oxford an old furry mouse which made a much better kitten than LT had done.

"You were very clever," Jack said.

Saturday modestly said nothing, but he could see that she agreed.

"Was it the Nose that did it?" Jack asked.

"It helped," Saturday said. "By the way, I didn't know your surname was Watson.

Not until my parents said it."

"So what?" Jack said.

"Well – Sherlock Holmes had a Watson. He helped with the easy bits. You can help me, if you want."

"With the detecting? Yes, *please*." Jack nearly fell off the wall in his excitement.

Saturday kicked her heels against the bricks. "Most detectives who aren't in the police call themselves private eyes." She paused and looked at Jack. "But I shall call myself the Private Nose."

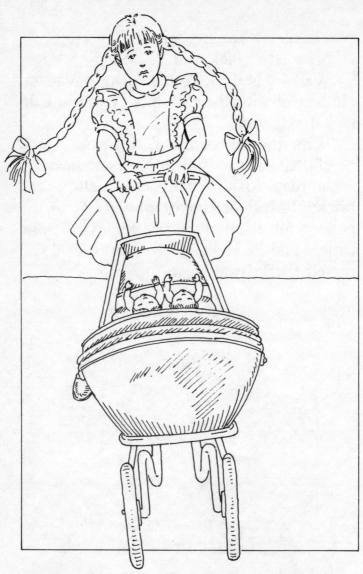

Behind the small pram was a small person who was wearing a pink dress and had very long pigtails.

THE CASE
OF THE
LITTLEJOHNS' GHOST

Jack Watson was lying on the grass reading a comic.

He was in the Holmeses' garden. Saturday Holmes, the great detective, was looking at a woodlouse through her brother's magnifying glass.

Something was squeaking in the distance. Saturday and Jack looked up. The noise grew louder. A small pram appeared by the front gate. Behind the small pram was a small person who was wearing a pink dress and had very long pigtails. On the ends of the pigtails were pink ribbons tied with big bows.

"Oh no!" Jack thought. "It's boring old Amelia Littlejohn."

"Hello," Saturday said. She got up and opened the gate.

Amelia wheeled in the pram. Inside the pram were her two dolls, Amanda and

Miranda. Amelia's eyes were red and her lips were trembling.

"Oh, Saturday," she said. "I need a Private Nose!"

Then she started to cry.

Saturday, who called herself the Private Nose because she had the Sherlock Holmes Nose for detection, asked what was wrong.

"It's the ghost!" Amelia wailed. "I saw it last night, and tonight it's coming to eat me!"

"I don't believe in ghosts," Saturday said. "You'd better tell me what happened."

Jack edged nearer. He was Saturday's assistant, and this sounded like a case for them.

"Ooh!" said Amelia. She stopped crying and bent over Amanda and Miranda. "Uncle Jack's come to say hello to you."

Jack blushed. "Oh, shut up," he said.

"Tell us about the ghost," Saturday said impatiently.

Amelia sat down on the front-door step, because the grass might be dirty. She put Amanda and Miranda on her lap.

"Well," she said. "You know my bedroom's downstairs, at the back of the house? I was going to sleep last night when I heard this whooing noise. *Whoo, whoo, whoo* – like that. It went on and on. Then the clanking started, like rattling chains. Ugh! And something scratched against the window, like a wild animal trying to get in."

Amelia started to cry again.

Saturday leant forwards. "It can't have been a ghost," she said firmly, "because ghosts aren't real. What happened next?"

"My...my curtains weren't quite closed." Amelia gulped. "Suddenly I could see this white shape, and it had two fiery eyes, and it was looking at me."

Jack glanced up at his own house, next door. Suppose the ghost should come and look through *his* bedroom window?

"How tall was it?" Saturday asked.

"I don't know," Amelia said. "Taller than a grown-up, probably. I was so scared I couldn't tell. Anyway, I was trying not to look at it. Then it spoke!"

Jack shivered.

Saturday looked interested. "Well? What did it say?"

Amelia's eyes grew big and round. "It said, 'Tomorrow I'm coming to eat you up, chomp, chomp, chomp. Tomorrow I'm coming to eat you up, chomp, chomp, chomp. Tomorrow – '"

"All right," Saturday said. "I heard you the first time. What was the voice like?"

"Sort of thick and throaty and...*hungry*!"

"What did you do?" Jack asked.

"I screamed and ran into the sitting room," Amelia said. "Daddy looked outside with his torch, but he couldn't see anything. He got a bit angry because Baby woke up and started crying. Mummy said I must have had a bad dream."

"Perhaps you did," Saturday said.

"I didn't!" Amelia shouted. "It was a *real* ghost!"

Saturday sighed. "What do you want me to do?" she asked.

"Catch it! You can catch crooks, so can't

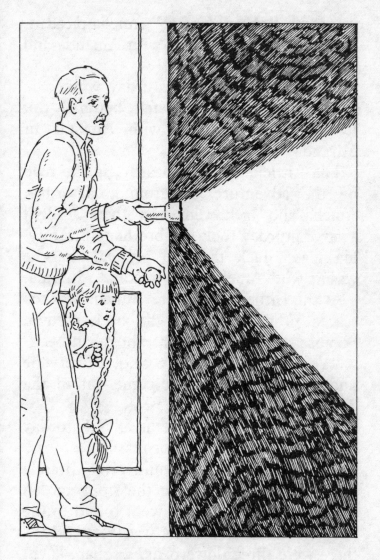

*"Daddy looked outside with his torch,
but he couldn't see anything."*

you catch a ghost? Go on," Amelia pleaded. "Please. I'll let you play with Amanda and Miranda."

"We'll investigate." Saturday winked at Jack, who immediately felt better. "But I don't want to play with Amanda or Miranda."

The Littlejohns lived nearby, in the road by the adventure playground. Saturday, Amelia and Jack went over there straight away. Saturday took her brother's magnifying glass. Jack tried to pretend that he wasn't with Amelia, Amanda and Miranda.

At the Littlejohns' house, Amelia was too scared to go round to the back garden, because that was where the ghost had been.

"You're a sissy," Jack said. "Everyone knows that ghosts don't come out in the daytime."

"They don't come out at all," Saturday said. "Because they're not real."

Amelia decided she would give Miranda and Amanda their tea in the front garden while Saturday and Jack went round to the back. The back garden was very tidy – there were three flowerbeds, a square lawn, a vegetable patch and a tool shed. Near the shed was a rusty dustbin full of dead leaves.

Saturday took out her magnifying glass and began to crawl over the lawn. It seemed to Jack as though she was looking at every blade of grass.

Jack looked around as well – he didn't see why he couldn't detect something too. But he couldn't find anything except grass and flowers and, after a while, he got bored. Saturday was still on her hands and knees.

"What are you looking for?" Jack asked.

"How can I know," Saturday said, "until I've found it?"

Jack chewed a piece of grass and stared around. On his right was a high brick wall; there was another road on the other side of it. On the left was a tall fence – horrible Nigel Knight and his horrible dog Stinker lived in the house beyond.

Next door to the Knights, was the Reillys' house, where Ryan lived. Ryan was a friend of Jack and Saturday's.

He wondered who lived beyond the hedge at the bottom of the Littlejohns' garden. He didn't recognise the house.

"Aha!" said Saturday. She had reached the part of the lawn which was closest to Amelia's bedroom window. "Come and look at this."

Jack rushed over to her. She pointed at two grey blobs on the grass. Neither was larger than Jack's little fingernail.

"What are they?" Jack asked. The blobs looked very unexciting.

"Clues," Saturday said. "Maybe Amelia didn't dream her ghost after all."

She scraped the blobs off the grass and put them in an envelope which she took from her pocket.

"Why are you doing that?" Jack said.

"You have to keep clues because they prove things."

Saturday refused to tell him why the blobs were important. She went on looking through her brother's magnifying glass. Now she was looking at the plants in the narrow flowerbed directly under Amelia's window.

"Aha!" she said.

Jack looked up. This time he didn't rush over. It wasn't worth rushing for little grey blobs.

Saturday pointed at the rose bush. "Can you see what's here? Hanging on that big thorn?"

Jack came over and had a look. "It's only a bit of white cotton," he said. Cotton was just as boring as little grey blobs.

Saturday shook her head. "It could be another important clue." She lifted the piece of thread from the thorn and put it in her envelope. "Come on, Jack. Let's look at the rest of the garden."

He trailed after her. She looked very carefully at the wall on the right and at the fence on the left. She looked even more carefully at the hedge at the end of the garden, especially at the part of the hedge which was half hidden by the tool shed.

"*Aha!*" she said, much more loudly than before.

Jack jumped with surprise.

"Come here," she said. "I've found *lots* of clues."

"I'm going to investigate," Saturday said.
She crawled through the hedge and disappeared.

They had to wriggle between the hedge and the shed. Saturday pointed at another bit of white cotton which dangled from one of the twigs in the hedge. More excitingly, there was a hole in the hedge. Jack looked through the hole and found he could see the wooden side of another tool shed. On the ground on the other side of the hole were two more grey blobs.

"Who lives there?" Saturday asked.

Jack shook his head. "I don't know."

"I'm going to investigate," Saturday said.

"W-what?" Jack said. "You're going through there?"

Saturday nodded. "Of course."

Jack hoped he didn't look as scared as he was feeling. After all, "through there" was probably where the ghost lived.

"I'll come with you," he said.

To his great relief, Saturday shook her head.

"No," she said. "I'd better go by myself, in case I don't come back. Then you can sound the alarm. Just wait here."

She crawled through the hedge and disappeared. Jack sat on the grass by the tool shed door and closed his eyes tightly. Suppose Saturday didn't come back? Would anyone believe him when he tried to raise the alarm? Suppose the ghost *ate* Saturday? Perhaps the ghost would even eat bones. He reminded himself that ghosts only came out at night but it no longer sounded as convincing as it had done when he said it to Amelia. Suppose –

There was a tap on his shoulder.

Jack gasped and opened his eyes.

Saturday grinned down at him. "You look as if you've seen a ghost!" she said. "Come on, I want to find Amelia."

Jack asked her what she had found out, but she wouldn't say.

Amelia was still giving her dolls their tea in the front garden.

"Have you caught the ghost, Saturday?" she asked. "Have some tea."

Amelia pretended to pour out two cups of tea; she put in pretend milk and sugar and held out the cups to Jack and Saturday. Jack put his down on the grass.

Saturday waved aside the other teacup. "I want some glue," she said. "Then I can deal with your ghost."

"Some *glue*?" Amelia said. "Whatever for?"

"Never you mind," Saturday said.

Amelia went into the house to ask her mother for some glue. In a few minutes she came back with a blue pot in her hand. Just as she came out, a very fat boy with rather long ginger hair came walking down the road towards the adventure playground. He said nothing, but he stuck out his tongue at Amelia.

"Ugh!" Amelia said as she gave the glue to Saturday. "That nasty rough boy's come back from his uncle's. I wish he'd stayed there for ever."

"What's his name?" Saturday said.

"That's Justin Badweather," Jack said.

"He lives in the house behind ours," Amelia said. "Anyway, here's the glue. Mummy said that it takes a long time to dry."

"Good," Saturday said, "that's just what

I wanted."

Saturday and Jack went back to the hole in the hedge by the tool shed. Amelia was still too scared to come into the back garden. Once again, Jack stayed on guard while Saturday wriggled through the hedge with the glue pot in her hand. A few minutes later she returned. She and Jack blocked the hole in the hedge with the old dustbin.

"That won't keep out a ghost," Jack said.

Saturday smiled. "It'll keep out this ghost," she said.

They gave back the glue to Mrs Little-john. Amelia wanted to know if they'd caught the ghost.

"Not exactly," Saturday said mysteriously. "But I don't think it'll be causing any more trouble. I'm going down to the playground now. Are you two coming?"

Jack said yes even though he didn't really want to because Justin Badweather would be there. Amelia said yes because she thought that Amanda and Miranda needed another outing in their pram.

*Saturday and Jack blocked the hole in
the hedge with the old dustbin.*

When they reached the playground, they found that everyone was standing around the oak tree. Justin Badweather was making a speech to them. Justin sent his friend Nigel Knight across to Saturday, Jack and Amelia, to tell them to come to listen to him.

"Well, I suppose we might as well go and listen," Saturday said. "We've got nothing better to do."

Justin looked at them as they came over. He sneered at Saturday; it was well-known that Justin thought all girls were soppy.

"I'm talking about our family ghost," he said importantly. His voice always sounded as if his nose was blocked. "It's my grandad. He died years ago, but people say his ghost still walks round here at night – looking for *food!*"

"Food?" said Amelia Littlejohn in a very shaky voice.

Justin nodded. "That's right. His favourite kind of food."

"And what's that?" Nigel asked.

"Children!" Justin sniggered. "Tasty little children. My grandad was a sailor, you see. One day he was shipwrecked. My grandad was alone on a raft with two young cabin boys. They had no food. They were rescued two weeks later. Or rather Grandad was. He was alone and two stone heavier, but the cabin boys were gone."

There was a moment of shocked silence. Justin licked his lips.

"After that," he said, "Grandad always ate children when he got the chance. The younger the better." His eyes rested on Amelia. "Especially little girls."

"Rubbish," said Saturday. "I don't see why girls should taste any different from boys. I don't believe in ghosts either. Only babies believe in ghosts."

"But I saw it last night," Nigel said. "It's dressed in white, and it's got eyes of fire and it clanks as it walks. Justin's grandad has come back to haunt us."

"You're making it up," Saturday said.

Nigel looked away. He was scared of Saturday.

"And who are you?" Justin said. "I don't

like new kids and I don't like girls."

"I'm Saturday Holmes. I'll make you a bet: the person who's pretending to be this ghost will have something wrong with their hair tomorrow morning. That's how we'll know who it is."

Justin's mouth fell open.

Nigel said to Justin in a loud whisper, "Better be careful. She's a detective."

"She's just a girl," Justin said. "I'm not scared of no girl. And Saturday's a stupid name."

"I dare you to come here tomorrow, all of you," Saturday said, "and see if I'm right."

"I was coming here tomorrow anyway," Justin said. "Tomorrow's Saturday, isn't it? Tell you what, I'm going to clean my shoes on Saturday. Ha, ha, *ha*!"

The next day everyone came to the adventure playground soon after breakfast. They had to come because Saturday had dared them. Also, they wanted to find out whether or not the ghost was real.

Jack was very worried. He couldn't see

Nigel said to Justin in a loud whisper,
"Better be careful. She's a detective."

*Saturday went round and looked
carefully at everyone's hair.*

how Saturday could prove that the ghost wasn't real. And if she couldn't, Justin would have his revenge on Saturday – and on Saturday's friends.

But Saturday wasn't worried. On their way to the playground they called for Amelia.

Amelia was very cheerful. "The ghost didn't come last night," she said happily.

"I didn't think it would," Saturday said.

As they passed the Reillys' house, Jack popped in to ask Ryan to come with them. Ryan was the only person he knew who was strong enough to stand a chance of beating Justin Badweather in a fight. That was one reason why Justin and Ryan were enemies.

The four of them arrived at the adventure playground. Everyone else was already there, except Justin Badweather.

"Never mind," Saturday said. "I can start without him."

She went round and looked carefully at everyone's hair. Jack couldn't understand why. Everyone's hair was exactly the same as it had been yesterday.

Nigel Knight said, "I told you so! The ghost is real!"

Suddenly Justin rode into the playground on his big red bike, ringing the bell on the handlebars. He stopped just inside the entrance, near where Ryan was standing. He had a very large check cap on his head.

"Can't stop," he said importantly, "I'm going out with my dad. Haven't got time for your silly games today. Watch out the ghost doesn't eat you!"

"Ryan!" Saturday shouted. "Knock his cap off!"

Ryan knocked off Justin's cap. Everyone except Justin started to laugh. Yesterday, Justin's ginger hair had been long and neatly cut. Now it was short and ragged.

Justin howled with rage, turned his bike and rode away as fast as he could.

Justin's friends edged away from Saturday and left the adventure playground. Everyone else came closer to her. She was standing by the oak tree, where Justin usually stood.

"I don't understand," Jack said. "How

did you do it?"

Saturday shrugged. "It was simple – Justin left so many clues that showed me he was the ghost. The bits of white cotton in Amelia's garden came from the sheet he wore. Those grey blobs were candle wax. When I went through the hedge, I found Justin's ghost disguise in the Badweathers' tool shed. There was an old sheet, a chain to make the clanking noises and a candle in an empty paint tin. He'd cut two holes in the side of the tin, which looked like two eyes in the darkness when the candle was lit. Nigel Knight must have been in the plot as well."

Ryan frowned. "But what happened to Justin's hair?"

"The sheet was pinned on to an old hat, so it wouldn't fall off." Saturday laughed. "I put the glue inside the hat. Anyone who tried to be a ghost would get glue all over his hair. I expect Justin's parents had to cut him out with scissors!"

*Jack leant out of bed and
rapped twice on the wall.*

THE CASE
OF THE
CAPTURED SHADOWS

Knock. Knock. KNOCK!

Jack Watson sat up in bed and yawned.

Knock. Knock. KNOCK!

Now which signal was that? Luckily the code was on the bedside table. "KNOCK! Knock. Knock": that meant "The enemy has captured me." Jack rubbed his eyes. Which enemy? That couldn't be right.

Knock. Knock. KNOCK!

He had got the wrong signal. "Knock. Knock. KNOCK!" meant "Meet me outside after breakfast." Perhaps Saturday had another case for them to solve.

Jack leant out of bed and rapped twice on the wall. That meant "Message received and understood." Saturday Holmes, the great detective, had the bedroom on the other side of the wall, in the house next door. It was her idea that they should use secret signals to keep in touch.

"Stop that banging!" Jack's father yelled from the next bedroom. "I'm asleep!"

After breakfast Jack went down to the bottom of the garden. Saturday was already sitting on the wall by the apple tree. Jack climbed up beside her.

"Is it a case?" he asked excitedly.

Saturday shook her head.

Jack felt a bit annoyed. If it wasn't a case, why had she signalled for him? Saturday was always being mysterious, even when she had nothing to be mysterious about.

"My brother was telling me about our ancestor Sherlock Holmes last night," she said. "When he'd solved a case, Watson used to say, 'Marvellous, Holmes! How on earth did you do it?' And then Holmes says 'Elementary, my dear Watson.' I think we should do that."

Jack frowned. "What does elly-whatever-it-was mean?"

"Elementary." Saturday looked down her nose at Jack, as if to say that he ought to have known what the word meant. "It means you don't understand it but I do. Or something like that."

"But what do you say if *I* solve a case?"

"But you won't, will you?" Saturday jumped down from the wall. "Come on, we've got to practise our detective skills. Let's shadow someone."

Jack nearly said that he wasn't going to come. How could Saturday be so sure he wouldn't solve a case? She was getting bigheaded. On the other hand, he had never shadowed anyone before, and it sounded interesting.

It was. First of all, they had to choose their disguises. Saturday borrowed her brother's blue jacket. It came down to her knees and it was far too warm for her, but it made her look different. She also wore a pair of sunglasses. Jack found an old straw hat which his mother used in the garden. It flopped over his ears. He carried a comic which he could pretend to be reading if he needed to hide the rest of his face.

Saturday made sure that they each had a piece of chalk. They might have to split up, and the one in front could draw arrows on the pavement to show the way. All they had to do now was choose someone to follow.

"It's better to follow someone who knows us," Saturday said. "It's harder, you see, and we can test our disguises. If we choose someone suspicious, it might even turn into a case for us."

They hid in Saturday's front garden, waiting for someone suspicious to go by. After a few minutes Mrs Grump came out of her house on the other side of the road. She snorted angrily at the weeds in Mr Patel's garden and waddled down the road.

"How about her?" Jack whispered. "She's suspicious all right."

Saturday nodded. "Everyone's scared of her, except me. And I bet she's not really that fat. I bet she's hiding stolen goods under her dress."

Saturday went first. Jack counted up to a hundred before he followed her. At the main road he found a chalked arrow which bent to the right. Mrs Grump must be going to the shops.

When Jack reached the shops he could see

*Mrs Grump snorted angrily at
the weeds in Mr Patel's garden.*

no sign of Mrs Grump. Saturday was standing outside a shoe shop; she seemed to be looking at some men's shoes.

Jack tapped her on the shoulder. Saturday jumped.

"Have you lost her?" he asked.

"Of course not! She's in the supermarket. I'm using the shoe shop window as a mirror, so I can watch the main entrance. If you go round the corner you can watch the side door. Find a shop window so she won't see it's you."

Jack went into the side street. There was a toyshop opposite the supermarket door. When he stared into its window he could see the door very clearly. He could also see himself; perhaps his mother's hat was a bit large for him.

He waited for what seemed like hours. At least he was outside an interesting shop. There was a big red dumper truck with a battery-powered electric motor and an orange light that flashed on and off. It looked expensive, but perhaps his parents would buy it for his birthday if he went without pocket money for a month.

Just as he was trying to read the price tag, he heard someone grunting behind him. He had been so interested in the toys that he had forgotten to look at the reflection. He glanced round. Mrs Grump was only a few feet away from him. Jack quickly put up his comic so she wouldn't recognize him.

Mrs Grump had a carrier bag in one hand and an airmail envelope in the other. She walked past Jack and into the post office beside the toyshop. Jack realized that he was holding the comic upside down. He was glad that Saturday wasn't there.

He peeped into the post office. Mrs Grump was waiting in one of the queues. He thought he could guess what she wanted. It was a long queue, so he had plenty of time to fetch Saturday.

She wasn't pleased, and said, "You should never leave a quarry." She rubbed her nose. "An airmail letter? A lot of crooks are international these days."

Jack said, "I expect she was sending it to – "

But Saturday wasn't listening. She was already running towards the post office. "I'll tail her now," she called over her shoulder. "You wait at the main road and follow me."

Jack shrugged. Saturday was too busy to listen to him. But she wasn't the only one who could have ideas. He stood on the corner and thought how wonderful it would be if he solved a case which had baffled Saturday.

Mrs Grump came out of the post office. She posted her letter and shuffled off in the opposite direction, away from where Jack was standing on the main road. Saturday came out of the post office and followed Mrs Grump. Jack followed Saturday.

The road twisted and turned. Jack lost sight of Saturday. When the road straightened out again, she was nowhere to be seen. But there was a chalk mark on the pavement by the gates of the Alderman Warlock Memorial Park.

Jack knew the park, though he didn't go there very often because it was so boring. It was full of flowerbeds and paths and benches. The trees were too small to climb and you weren't supposed to walk on the grass. The gardener hated dogs and children.

Saturday was crouching beside a litter bin. Between the gates and Saturday was a puddle. Jack walked through the water so he could see his footprints on the dry path.

"Don't do that!" Saturday said. "A good shadow never leaves tracks, in case he's being shadowed."

"How was I to know?" Jack demanded. "You never told me that."

"Sssh! Look, the quarry's over there."

Mrs Grump was talking to the gardener. They were too far away for the detectives to be able to hear what they were saying.

"She's probably telling him where she's going to leave the stolen goods. You know, the ones under her dress. I expect he passes them on to someone else. He looks like a crook."

When Mrs Grump moved away, Saturday allowed Jack to be the first to follow her.

The gardener looked at him very suspiciously as he passed. He said something that sounded like *Grrr!*

Mrs Grump left the park by the little gate behind the war memorial. Jack followed her into a street of gloomy red brick houses. There were cars parked along the road, so Jack had plenty of cover. Jack didn't recognize the street at first. But one of the houses had a little tower, with stained-glass windows. It looked like a castle. He was almost sure he had seen it before.

Mrs Grump turned into another street. Jack made a chalk mark on the pavement for Saturday. He peered round the corner. The houses here were smaller and even gloomier. Mrs Grump stopped, looked round and went into one of the gates near the end of the road.

Jack ran after her. You could hardly see the house (which was number thirteen) because the hedge was so big and untrimmed. There was a FOR SALE notice in the garden. Mrs Grump had just put a key in the front door. Jack suddenly remembered the one

*The gardener looked at Jack
very suspiciously as he passed.*

*Jack gulped, climbed on to the low
wall and jumped into the hedge.*

time he had been here before, to this very house.

"Aha!" Saturday whispered. She had come up very quietly behind him. "I thought so. An empty house – it's either the gang's headquarters or where they leave secret messages for one another."

"But – " Jack began.

The front door closed.

"Quick, there's no time to lose," Saturday interrupted. "I'll stay here and watch the front. You scout round to the back of the house. They may try and escape that way."

"They?" Jack said.

"There may be more than one of them. Go on. You're not scared, are you?"

Jack was, but of course he couldn't admit it. Everyone was scared of Mrs Grump. He gulped, climbed on to the low wall and jumped into the hedge.

It was fortunate that no one had done any gardening in that garden for months. In places the grass was as high as Jack's waist. The thick hedge ran along the side of the house, as well as the front, so Jack was able to crawl between it and the wall. He cut his knee twice, and once he ran into some nasty stinging nettles. But he reached the back garden without being spotted by Mrs Grump. He took cover behind an apple tree and watched the back door.

Mrs Grump loomed up on the other side of the kitchen window and jerked it open. She said, "Pah! The filth!" and disappeared again.

A minute later Jack heard a bang. It sounded like someone in a temper closing the front door.

Saturday ran up the path by the side of the house. Jack waved his hat to show her where he was. She flopped down beside him.

"Phew!" she said. "That was a narrow escape. She came out so fast that she nearly caught me. I had to dive into the hedge. I've torn my brother's jacket. Still, now's our chance to find out what she's up to."

"But – "

"You're not still scared, are you?" Saturday stood up. "I'm sure there's no one else in the house. I've been watching it like a hawk."

"No," Jack said. "It's not that. It's – "

"Come on. She's opened the little kitchen window. I bet I can stretch a hand in and open the big one beside it."

"But – "

It was too late. Saturday didn't want to listen to him. She was already climbing on to the windowsill. She reached in and tugged open the handle of the big window. Then she swung herself into the kitchen. Jack followed her in.

"We must move fast," Saturday said. "Keep your eyes peeled for clues. What's that on the floor? Look! It's blood!"

"I know," Jack said glumly. "It's mine."

He had cut his knee as he hauled himself over the sill.

"Then wipe it up with your tee shirt," Saturday hissed. "*We* mustn't leave clues."

The house had been stripped of furniture. In the hall was Mrs Grump's carrier bag. Saturday looked in it and found some floor cloths, a new dustpan and brush and a big bottle of disinfectant.

"She's going to clean up the house and get rid of all the fingerprints and things," she said. "We're just in time."

They looked quickly in each room. All they found were bare boards and peeling wallpaper. Saturday ran up the stairs with Jack close behind her. The front bedroom was empty. But on the floor of one of the back bedrooms was a yellowing newspaper, folded open at the crossword.

"Aha!" Saturday scooped it up. "Look, only two clues have been written in. You'll never guess what they are."

Jack came closer. "What?"

"One word is POLICE and the other is DISAPPEAR. It's a message, Jack. It means 'The POLICE are on to us. We'd better DISAPPEAR.' Clever, isn't it?"

"But perhaps those words are just the answers," Jack said.

Saturday frowned. "'Course they aren't. Here's the clue for the POLICE one: 'Work about the insects for the law.' If that means POLICE I'll eat your hat. The other one, for DISAPPEAR, is 'Vanish in hades – a quiet fruit.' That doesn't make sense either. So it must be a secret message."

"But – "

Downstairs, something rattled. The front door banged. A bolt shot back. A muffled "Pah!" floated up the stairs.

Saturday and Jack stared at each other with terror in their eyes. Mrs Grump had trapped them.

"Pah! All this dirt!"

Mrs Grump, muttering to herself, began to use the dustpan and brush. Every few seconds, her muttering and the scrape of the brush grew a little louder.

Saturday put her mouth to Jack's ear. "She must be coming up the stairs," she whispered. "Tiptoe behind the door."

One of the floorboards creaked as they moved, but Mrs Grump appeared not to notice. Jack's heart was pounding so loudly in his chest that he was sure it could be heard all over the house. He tried not to

They no longer bothered hurtled down the stairs, to keep quiet. They taking three at a time.

think about what would happen when she caught them. It would probably be even worse than the time Justin Badweather beat him up in the playground. And afterwards she would tell their parents.

Saturday clutched Jack's arm. Mrs Grump had reached the landing. Jack could see her through the crack between the door and the wall. She was panting, and wiping her forehead. She turned and went into the bathroom. There was a gush of running water as she filled up a bucket.

"Quick!" Saturday whispered. "Run!"

They no longer bothered to keep quiet. They hurtled down the stairs, taking three at a time. Saturday tugged at the front door but it was locked. Jack ran for the kitchen with Saturday at his heels.

"Who's there?" Mrs Grump was pounding down the stairs, bouncing like a big black ball. "Stop thief! Police!"

The door into the kitchen had jammed. Saturday couldn't get it open. Mrs Grump still hadn't seen them, but it could only be a matter of seconds.

Then Jack had a brainwave. He opened a little door which was half hidden under the stairs. He grabbed Saturday by the wrist and plunged with her into the darkness beyond.

Jack pushed the door shut behind them. With any luck, Mrs Grump would think it was the sound of the kitchen door being shut.

It was completely dark. Jack bit his lip and waited.

"Pah!" Mrs Grump shouted in triumph on the other side of the door. There was a *click!* as she locked them in. "Got you! You won't get out of there in a hurry! We'll see what you have to say to the police! I hope you go to jail!"

The front door banged. The darkness settled around them like a blanket. Saturday tried the door. It was well and truly locked.

She sniffed. "But we're detectives," she said. "We're on the same side as the police. And if she's a crook, why's she going to the police?"

Saturday sniffed again.

*Jack grabbed Saturday by the wrist and
plunged with her into the darkness beyond.*

Jack coughed. For once he felt as if he was older than Saturday rather than the other way round.

"Put your hand on my shoulder," he said. "We're going down some steps."

Saturday followed him meekly. It was cool in the cellar. At the bottom of the stairs, Jack felt for the wall. Using that as a guide, he worked his way round the cellar, with Saturday close behind him. As he walked, he rapped on the wall. The brick made very little sound.

But suddenly there was the dull boom of wood. Jack reached up and found the bolts. They were stiff and rusty but he managed to draw them back. Then he pushed. The square of wood fell back and light flooded into the cellar.

Jack pulled himself up into one of the bushes at the side of the house.

"Come on," he said to Saturday. "There's no time to waste. Ow! Mind the nettles!"

Mrs Grump was talking to Jack's mother over the Watsons' gate.

"You could have knocked me down with a feather," Mrs Grump screeched. "There were two burglars. I only caught a glimpse of them, out of the corner of my eye. Huge, evil-looking men. I think they wore masks. But they didn't get much change out of me. Pah! I locked them in the cellar and called the police from next door."

"So they've been arrested?" Mrs Watson asked.

Mrs Grump wobbled with indignation. "The police took hours! I could have been murdered! By the time they arrived, the crooks had escaped. Pah!"

"Did they find any clues?" Mrs Watson asked.

"I found the clues," Mrs Grump said firmly. "Two of them. A pair of sunglasses and a great big straw hat. 'You mark my words,' I told the police, 'those burglars are foreigners.'"

Jack, who had been standing on his head behind his mother's back and pretending not to listen, turned himself the right way up and walked quietly down the path to the back garden.

Saturday was already waiting on the wall. They hadn't had time to talk since their escape. They had split up and gone home as quickly as possible, by different ways.

"You were wonderful, Jack," she said. "I mean, it was dark in that cellar. You must have x-ray eyes."

Jack climbed up the apple tree and sat beside her on the wall. For a moment he wondered if he should tell her everything. He had tried to tell her several times, but Saturday just wouldn't listen. He could have told her that Mrs Grump's married sister had gone to Australia last winter, and that Mrs Grump was always sending her airmail letters; that they used to live in that empty house near the park; that Jack had gone there once, for the birthday party of Mrs Grump's nephew; that they'd played hide-and-seek all over the house; and that he knew all about the empty cellar, because Justin Badweather had left the party early through the old coal hatch, taking the birthday cake with him.

"How on earth did you do it?" Saturday asked.

Jack smiled mysteriously. "Elly...er, elementary," he said. "Elementary, my dear Holmes."